Wounded

LaTrice Marie

ISBN 978-1-64140-071-8 (Paperback)
ISBN 978-1-64140-072-5 (Digital)

Christian Faith Publishing, Inc.
296 Chestnut Street
Meadville, PA 16335
www.christianfaithpublishing.com

Printed in the United States of America

Mission Statement

The mission of LaTrice Marie is to equip readers and followers with divine wisdom and understanding that no matter what their current situation is, God is still able and willing to deliver. He is the king that resides within us and still performing the same miracles that we read about in the Bible. It is our responsibility to reach out and receive what He is offering. It is my goal to inspire and instill greatness that will result in deliberate actions, plans, and focus on becoming whom we were purposed to be. It is my aim to ignite a fire that will allow us to bless others through mentoring and motivating our youth. For I am a true believer, and I acknowledge that we are our brothers' and sisters' keepers…

F irst off, I'd like to give thanks to my Lord and personal Savior that continues to bless, heal, restore and deliver me. Knowing that at times (and many occasions) I am not deserving of His time and attention, He still blesses me to have the perfect people at my side.

With that being said, I would like to take the time to thank my mother, Betty, for doing the very best that she could with what she knew, trusted and believed. I also must make mention of my beloved children, Roderick (Timmi) and Robynn, who bring an electric element of love to my life that exemplifies all that I would like to become in order to bless and show them what potential is housed within them. You are my pulse and the rhythm of my breathing. I love you all more than you could ever collectively imagine (period). I thank God that He blessed me with and for you. Never be afraid to step out and secure your dreams as God gave them to you and will be your guide along the way.

In addition, I want to show appreciation to my cousin, Printella. She not only demonstrates great leadership but also took me under her wings. Prin has shown me that I can brilliantly fly solo as long as I am willing to believe and take the appropriate steps of faith. Giving respect where it is due, it is essential that I thank Prudencia for not only believing in me and the dream that I am chasing but also for countless hours of pushing, proof reading, and being the vested support system that I needed, trusted, and leaned on from time to time. Thank you!

To my precious prayer warriors, Erica and Nicolette, you have been more than a blessing to me. You have been or given the answer to many sincere silent prayers. Thus, I know that the Lord works with and through you both. You have been like teachers that I could never repay for your time and dedication. I thank you for loving me and taking the time to show me how to pray earnestly.

To my step dads who played a pivotal role in my life (Bruce C. Jacobs (RIP), Winston, and Robert (aka Shark)), sisters (Nickee, Whitney, Brittney and Shavon) along with my niece (Danni) and nephews (Christian, David and SaVon), I love every bit of craziness that I encounter when I am in your presence. You inspire me to do better, chase harder, and give my all. To Rochelle, I thank you for setting the example on how to love family in an outward fashion. To Johnny and Juanita, I have learned so much from you two and appreciate everything in totality. To Edith, I thank you for allowing me to barrow your smile and your spirit in order to show the world that there is still kindness and gentility in places that we least expect it. To Cari (Anthony) and Willie, continue to thrive, motivate and instruct as you are leaders and pour out blessings among His people. Now it's your time and season to reap the harvest.

In closing, I would also hate to fail to mention my Pastor Dennis and Evangelist Fulmore (COTLG, Deerfield). I love you, your ministries and your worship. May the Lord continue to bless you openly in abundance. To my family, friends and everyone that I encountered along the way, I thank and dedicate this book to you in love…

Romans 8:18

For I reckon that the sufferings of this present time are not worthy
to be compared with the glory which shall be revealed in us.

Chapter 1

I 'm walking home alone as the crowd gathers behind me sneering, chanting and fighting for the first swing at me. Oh God! I feel my skin getting clammy as my balance begins to waver unjustly under the surmounting weight from within my chest. All of a sudden, I'm light-headed and my vision has seemingly blurred. "One day," I say aloud as I begin to hope and pray for immediate serenity from my daily predators. I need for them to tire and grow bored with this inevitable cruel game of mocking me. But what can I do to prevent this brutal battle that taints not only my life but my self-image as well?

For years, my teachers have told me to ignore my persecutors because I'm much better off than they are. On the other hand, my mother challenges me daily, "If they hit you, then grab one and stomp them back until their mother feels it!" As she spits these flagrant words in my direction, I can't help but feel the hurt and embarrassment barreling in her voice which attempts to mask anger. "How could you allow…" Silence. Peace, finally its mine. Her lips move frantically in a feverish fashion and yet I hear nothing.

Here it is Monday, and I am praying for Saturday and Sunday to fall gracefully upon us like now. I hear the mob approaching quickly and I leap back into action forgetting the day-mare invading my life and current thought pattern. Even though I am permitted to leave school 10 minutes prior to dismissal, my short, frail limbs have failed me yet again. I muster just enough courage to wince over my right shoulder to see that the crowd is larger than before and gaining on me like flies to fresh dung. I cling to my book-bag like a patient clings to life support and plead with my legs to move faster, grow longer and push harder in the direction of my house.

Oh please, please, please. I need divine intervention and I need it now. I need to be swept away from the here and now of this poisonous atmosphere. Just as soon as I move to dart in the other direction (shake them so I think), I feel a pang slap dab in the very center and back of my head. I lose momentum and land face first on the cement which absorbs most of the blow. I hear a violent thunder of laughter exploding around me before the blackness swallows me and bids me goodnight.

I'm freezing cold, wet and my body feels as though it's been trampled by horses. I try for what seems like hours just to raise my head from this concrete jungle now plastered to my face. Every ounce of me is shattered as the rain falls heavily upon the ground and my person. Unsure of the time but certain that my mother's anger is mounting uncontrollably due to my absence. I struggle with all of my might to a four-legged position. That's when I realize that both of my shoes have been removed. "Not again," I shout as the rain silences my fears and frustrations momentarily. I know without a shadow of doubt that taking my shoes was as malicious act to flog me continuously with humiliation at the beat down war-torn SX-500s I was wearing earlier…

In an awkward and disheveled manner, I navigate home fully aware that no matter how well I attempt to prepare for battle with mom, I will lose! My mother's vicious words and manner will cannibalize my spirit and smear my flesh with welts that travel endlessly over my body. My stomach curls and ties in a multitude of knots. My head hurts like my body is busted and yet it's my sanity that is spiraling into splinters too foreign to recognize. The remaining fragments are shaded heavily with the intent for revenge. Not how but, in fact, when is the only question I currently have.

I take one last, deep continuous breath as I enter my yard. My dog, Bullet, is tethered on his walking leash to a tree posted in front of the house. As I make my way over to him, he merely turns his head in the other direction as if I haven't been gone all day. His actions nearly cripple me with a cautionary glaring to be very careful of what's waiting for me within the walls of my home. I know it's going down in the worst of ways and yet it's too late to turn back and change strokes midstream. I keep it moving and walk into the house in my soggy, blackened socks and feign felicity in seeing my mother's face.

"Hi mom! I," before I could finish my statement, the phone escapes my mother's grasp and crashes to the floor. "I can explain! Mom wait! Please." I fight to cough, breathe, think and shout as her powerful hands surrounds and squeeze my larynx like the trigger of a small gun. My eyes feel swelling as the heat multiplies behind them and tears growl from their sockets uncontrollably. At this point, I am more than certain that they not only can but will leap forcefully from my face and hit the ground.

Aiming to communicate my thoughts, all I can conger up are high-pitched squeals that ignite the back of my throat with fire. Breathing has elapsed and darkness encircles me like crows to carcass stranded on empty highways. "Mommy, please," I try to express telepathically as I attempt to will her into looking deep into my wounded, fragile eyes and scorned soul. I find myself praying to a Heavenly Father that I've been told does not even exist that she finds something new and appeasing in my bewildered eyes. I pray that she finds a morsel of love staring back sharply in her focus before my eyes close in permanence to her unforgiving grip-locked hands around my neck…

I fall to the earth and it feels more forgiving and nurturing than her touch ever was upon my person. *Why does she hate me so much*, I find myself asking yet again? Knowing full well that I will never have the courage to ask her this aloud, I smile inwardly assured that this attack too is now over. Surprisingly, I have survived by the slightest of margins. At this very instance, I am rudely torn from this delusional sense of safety net by the repeat thudding sound delivered viciously upon my ribs from her unyielding kicks followed by more flagrant words foaming from her lips. My thoughts are now muffled and confusingly distorted and yet I feel no pain. Only the numbness throbbing from my thoughts and body consume me as I curl into the protective letter "c" under her feet.

I lay in the ground like a possum, but only broken. I am soundless, motionless and endless replications in thought-building process which leads me nowhere fast. Unanswered are my questions and attempts to unconditionally love my abuser with the velvetest of names, Mommy. Currently, the name stains my lips leaving the vividly severe and grotesque taste on my tongue. The name renders my spirit tarnished and void of positive affluence in character. Amazingly, I still live to love her. Every moment in every day, I secretly yearn for her to render a kind word, a soft supple kiss or an unshakable hug both intentional and gently planted upon me. Infinitely, I seem to be waiting and countless are the hours spent longing to be validated by her benevolence.

Simultaneously, I find myself wondering if I had a father, what he would be like. Would he love and caress me? Would he teach me the lessons of life that only he could? Fantastic fantasies begin to form dancing carelessly through my mind before the intruder enters thick-rooted shadow first. "Kill them all," he says failing to conceal his excitement. His head is down but I can feel his shifty, tar-colored, emotionless eyes piercing ever so callously into me. "Start with her," he demands pointing with his chin towards my mother as he juggles her gun from one palm to the next.

My rebuttal is weak and I stutter hopelessly, "I, I could never do that to her." It is more of a question than a declaration and somehow I know that the intruder can feel it more than I. "She loves me." I whisper making sure not to announce it too loudly and brilliantly offend her yet again today.

My objective is to disguise the pain and anguish that color me emotionally damaged. I intend to sound convincingly cool and calm but flunk horribly to my very own dismay. The shadow crouching before me simply laughs boisterously like thunder and diffuses at the sound of my mother's voice. "Who the hell are you talking to?" She calls from the kitchen. I dare not answer her for safety's sake and curl back into a ball as my body continues to tremble uncontrollably. "That's it dumb ass. Go straight to bed without dinner and maybe next time you'll decide to come home immediately after school," she shrieks as I hear the Johnny Walker bottle thump familiarly upon the table.

I rise early the next morning and peek out into the world from under the protective fortress I call my bed. I am delighted to find that I am not only safe but just as surprisingly dry too. I can't remember the last time this occurred but I can't wait to see her today. Believe it or not, I'm thrilled about going to school and seeing the one true person that cares for me, Ms. Seiko. She's my sixth-period teacher and my light glowing at the end of the darkest tunnel. She is who I run to in my dreams, my shelter in the storms castrating me daily. She is the softest caress, pat on the back and sweetest words of encouragement distributed. She may just be the very reason that I intend to repeat my current grade again.

I may not know love personally but transcend in the joy that she gorges me with in her presence. My heart shows out like the majorettes at the beginning of a Holiday parade every time that she enters my peripheral. I am endlessly speechless. I am weightless, yet full of light and hope. Her lips coil and I smile with an animated glow radiating from my desk. All that I am at these very moments is confident that my eyes are screaming the anticipation brewing within as she looks down upon me. She penetrates my soul with adoration and I long to consume every ounce of her time whether it be good, bad or indifferent. Mentally, she is mine in this empty room we share among trespassers…

I spend most of my spare time thinking of her and the brief moments we have shared in class. Her smile, sweet aroma and encouraging words make me momentarily appreciate being born. When I look at her, I can only see myself. I levitate into a successful adult (excuse me), woman, unlike the tangled mess I am as a teen. My eyes and whole being beg for her to call on me to deliver the answer that

I hold on to and she needs to hear in order to feel appreciated and most importantly, heard.

Conversely, when she does, I act as though I am clueless of the answers that she is trying to purge from the class. Believe it or not, in most cases, I know the answers like I know my name. And yet I refuse to draw attention to myself, outdated clothing or occasional putrid smell of stale urine saturating my flesh from the previous night. I totally acknowledge the fact that I need to get this horrendous thing under control since like third grade, but it remains simply out of my reach for some odd reason.

I practically break into a sprint to relieve myself in the unoccupied bathroom of my home when the pain erupts heavily from every direction of my body. Instant and abruptly, I am snapped back into this intense and cruel reality. I slowly lift my t-shirt to find that my ribs and stomach are matted with purple bruises running rampantly in unison along my torso. The sting is so loud that I want to plug my ears and vomit until the feeling dissipates. Mystified and infuriated, I find my eyes raised to an exclamation at the ring plastered uncaringly around my neck by the devil her friggin' self. Instantaneously or so it seems, my overwhelmingly concentrated hate for her magnifies to a limitless degree igniting my pulse to one continuous and thunderous loud beat.

My eyes spring leaks and mirror the weight plundered in my heart. I stare blankly at the mortified dark-eyed girl staring back at me. She's of average height but slightly obese. She is not pretty nor can she romanticize about being marginally attractive. Her eyes and ears are both large and devour the majority of her pitiful face. Her top lip is painfully thin while her lower lip is full and appears to spread sarcastically too close to the edges of her face. Contrarily, her slender nose remains inconsistent with the rest of her unremarkable features and sparks warranted ridicule on a regular basis. Her irises are stained with gloom and impenetrable. Grief traces circles under her eyes so ripe that they appear ready to bust and yet no one seems to take notice. Daily, she questions the reasoning for her birth and the logic for the heartache impaling her so intensely daily.

I begin to slowly swat away the tears spilling against my cheeks in an attempt to blot away the anger manifesting rapidly from within. I step warily away from the mirror not liking the image blaring miserably back at me. It was as if my reflection was mocking my very existence. My mismatched lips are as dry and cracked as my motivation to continue on this twisted journey in life alone. Reality is biting me incessantly and drains pleasantries from my soul, temperament and fraudulent smile.

I walk to the living room closet and grab a black scarf to wrap around my newly acquired bruises as I am morbidly interrupted by the forced groans coming from my mother's room. She is attempting to fake an orgasm that seems to be prolonged and exaggerated to no avail. *Not again*, I think and twist my eyes full blast behind my lids. I wonder what bill is facing termination this week and driving her to seek shelter under the grunter infesting my space and permeating my thoughts with remorse. I know for certain that it's not the married man, Cordell, that she is sightlessly in love with for her sounds would be harmonious, light and overflowing with beautiful expressions.

By any means necessary, she bends, folds and caters to his every whim simply suggested. For him, she is soft, forgiving and enthusiastically giving her all. For him, she is the totality of love, serenity, and uninterrupted joy. For me, she is short-tempered, hostile and curses my birth. Her actions speak volumes and paint us as polar opposites. Last month, I witnessed her "loan" him the rent money without a moment's hesitation or thought. Two weeks later, we had an eviction notice posted on the front door, no food in the fridge or cabinets and he was nowhere to be found. Not only did he refrain from returning or answering her calls, but I in turn I suffered the worst beating ever. Shortly thereafter, she started turning tricks like her first name was Circus.

The rent was then paid, he was forgiven and everything went back to normal as if nothing detrimental had ever transpired. Cordell continues to serve his unipurpose in her life by keeping her smiling and gratified in their language of love that penetrates the walls in our humble establishment. At the end of their daylong feastings upon each other, she is guaranteed to burst into a cantankerous giggle that continues to haunt me in remembrance. Amazingly, his actions and their sounds trace an abundance of happiness temporarily into my character.

On those days, she stays playfully in her room, body glistening on soaked sheets staring aimlessly into his eyes. When our paths do cross, she looks at me as if I'm tolerable and no longer a sharpened thorn in her side. These are the days I cherish most in life. I stay locked up in my room savoring every detail in my mom's romance novels. At seventeen, I am very much so addicted and would consider myself a scholar of their teachings. I cling to every strand unfolded during those days and dread closing my eyes and recklessly concluding my provisional ecstasy. Knowing that his visits are short-lived as he must return home to his naïve wife and deserving kids, I fight back tears as I hear my mother whimper and plead for him to stay as if she was unaware that time would come and devastated that it has.

As I shut the closet door behind me, I am blasted yet again with my mother's mutilated moaning. I am currently posted between her room and front door hesitant to move. The springs on her bed sound as if she is being hammered by a band of wrestlers going hard for a chance at the title. She sounds both labored and grotesque as she pleads for him to end the atrocity being deposited between her legs. I am simultaneously bewildered and absorbed by this moment. I am unsure if I should stay or if I should go as she continues to beg for him to stop. I am catapulted at this very moment with grief and positively certain that something is magnificently wrong. I press my backside against the door and slide helplessly to the floor closing my eyes and rocking myself into a silent quiver…

Uncertain of the length of time that has elapsed, I open my eyes as I hear his last plunge into my mother's womb. "Ohhh!!!" He yells shakily at the top of his lungs. "That's right! Suck it off." She sighs and I hear her room explode in heckling as the door slams open. One tall, dark-haired white man staggers out zipping his pants up and stumbles over me. He then reaches into his pocket and tosses a wad of money carelessly back into the room. As I turn ever so slightly towards the room, I see Cordell. In a wringing fashion, he's wiping his penis off on my mother's bloody sheet. Our eyes lock while my jaw hits the floor and shatters.

I scramble to my feet and stare blankly into the room at my mother's delicate disposition. His blazing smile abruptly interrupts and enunciates my fears. I am paralyzed by this display of approval as he smacks my mother on the bare bottom and commands her to turn over on her back. Never looking in my direction, she does as she is told. He forcefully drops the sheet exposing a large erect missile and then licks her lips in a dangerously provocative manner.

Cordell grasp her by the neck in order to maintain his balance and uses his knees to jar her legs apart in front of me. Mother is sprawled out helplessly naked at the corner of her very own mattress being flogged. Never missing a beat, he inserts the tip of his cannon in a circular motion and begins thrusting frantically inside her limp body. Her head rolls inadvertently in my direction exposing her empty dilated pupils. He slows momentarily as if checking for my reaction and ignites another attack.

I am plummeting like the captain of a recent shipwreck. I proceed in a downward spiral as he barrels his spiritless eyes deeply into my soul. Subsequently, he begins staring at me with hunger in his eyes so thick I could taste his excitement from across the room. He begins to whisper in gradual sweet slow breaths, "Come here babe, please!" In between long harsh silence, he continues, "I need you. Don't be scared." He pleads with me as misery settles righteously in my heart.

Unexpectedly, his speed quickens and I remain glued in a trance as he begins grunting wildly like a caged animal pleading for escape. His manic stare is never broken from my eyesight which exposes his new state of vulnerability. I witness this barbaric beast descend into a pathetic organism before my very eyes. Sliding tenderly unto my mother's breast, he looks breakable and saturated with regret. But how can I be certain that he is genuine at this point? A singular tear is shed from his socket and I now know with certainty that I am free to move.

Unsteadily, I tear away from the strong grip he has cast upon me. However, I cannot rid myself of the monstrosities rendered ruthlessly against my mother. Like a shadow chasing the night, I'm weightless in strength and execution. I am the moment of his destruction waiting to happen. After experiencing such a magnificent blow in life, I should be critically loud. In spite of this, I remain confused and redundantly silent. I have just witnessed the beast feasting malevolently on the woman who professes to love him most. I want to flee from this situation and destroy all memories tying me here and yet my sneakers stick solidly to the floor as nausea turns my stomach against me.

Chapter 2

I am muffled screams of victims everywhere stuck in lose, lost situations. I am disdained taste and scorned intensions united in the dark paths. I am violent trembles like my mother's head bobbing uncontrollably under his weight. I am defeated journeys of proper steps never initiated at haunting hours. I am the cruel blade of karma twisting and jabbing wickedly at his spine for her revenge...

Where should I turn when I have darkness erupting like volcanoes in my heart, madness exploiting my memories and revenge pulsing through my veins? I stare aimlessly from the ceiling back to my mother as I sit crouching in the corner of her room. I still see him invading my mother like gold-diggers after a funeral in the home of the departed. I can still hear him and smell the dampness on his cheek. It's like a vulture awakening on the inside of me waiting to attack a slow, wounded prey. I know not who I am at this very moment let alone what I will do if/when I see him again. I cry not for my mother (once more) but for my innocence that was shed like snake's skin two nights ago. She moans and I am now stuck in the today that we are now facing separately. We are merged together like the night of day meeting light.

Her eyes open and mourn louder than the tears hammering the fresh pillowcases I put on. Our eyes exchange whispers that replicate the daggers imploding within the confines of our hearts. We share this moment, hurt and crucifixion simultaneously and singularly in silence for an eternity or so it seems... My only resurrecting thought is exploiting his weakness which I am beginning to sip on spiritually. I'm beginning to understand that it's me that he wants. And it's me that he will get, unadulterated, unleashed and unremorseful. I will rein spores of destruction heavily upon every aspect of his person. Every spare second of each day, I will single-handedly manifest malevolent manifestations of his obliteration light-heartedly with a smile stemming from my soul. Her assailant's annihilation is now interchangeable with my first name, Destiny…

I am now disrupted with a burning desire to hold, rock and kiss my mother which seems mockingly unnatural. However, the fear of rejection and denial is the greater of these two feelings. Instinctively, I rise to my knees and pull away from both her and these foreign impulses. As I turn to exit the room, I hear her call my name between sobs. I'm inclined to pretend as though I had not heard her which momentarily hardens my heart. Her vulnerability both alters and alleviates my apprehensive steps toward the door.

I can no longer look at her or respond aloud. I drag one long breath in and almost forget to exhale as I wait endlessly for her to continue. Inwardly, I am trembling and unraveling uncontrollably. Outwardly, I appear to stand tall and confident in her presence for the first time. My subconscious, in turn, is folded and in dire need of renovation. "Destiny Ann," she finally musters. This is followed by yet another elongated silence and then more weeping. In my peripheral vision, I can see her out-stretched arm reaching for me. The internal dam is shattered and I depart, violently slamming the door behind me vowing to never again look back or cry.

I enter the school yard a newly empowered creature. I refuse to be tormented from this day forward. I will ignore all scornful word-plays but not one hair on this body will be shifted via someone else. I solemnly pledge in silence to make every attempt to disguise the recent remnants of hatred broiling cruelly close to my surface. I will remain in control of every outcome, situation and self on this day onward. I feel more than dangerous at this moment. I feel deadly and I am fighting aimlessly to contain it. The seams of my person are bursting from the fiery patches within. I am like a cannonball waiting for dispatch or a trigger waiting to bust. It's beginning to terrify even me because I have already caught glimpses of froggish cowards waiting to leap.

I suck my teeth and go into the office and fetch a late slip and receive the third degree for another series of unexcused absences for free. I never respond to the Dean's line of questioning or even blink at the empty threats being flung throughout the office. I am blank and darkness united. Both are staining more than my sunken eyes and heart at this early hour of the morn. I can feel the darkness pursuing and suffocating a host of victims plotting their attack against me. Impatiently, I await this pivotal moment and game-changing, inevitable event.

I hear the late bell ring as I exit the office and head towards my third-period class. I scamper into the empty hallways feeling as though I am being sought after. I quickly glimpse over my shoulder and realize that there is nothing and no one lingering behind. I enter the classroom full of empty faces staring back in my direction. I place the tardy slip on my teacher's desk and sliver quietly into the first available seat. Initially, my intentions were to simply disappear into self and regroup. Before I initiate this plan of action, my cheek is splattered with something cold, slimy and wet in the form of a ball.

One deep, long lasting breath is stolen from my lungs as it is heaved to the ground. I am physically frozen in the moment, questioning, *Why me, now, and how much more can I endure?* I begin grinding my teeth and chanting my new positive affirmations silently. Putting my head down, I start slowly. *I have total control. I will not give them what they both deserve and seek after. I will not allow them to bear witness to my major mental meltdown in the middle of class. I will not lash out impulsively like an enraged animal being taunted from behind fragile glass.*

As luck would have it, before these positive thoughts could manifest into personal beliefs, I hear soft footsteps quickening in my direction. The tension and atmosphere in the room are equally thicker than two wool sweaters and yet I remain locked protectively between two forearms. I am alert, perplexed and afraid to a whole new level as my passive nature is beginning to crumble. I am shaking nervously with anticipation rising as I am certain that something unpleasant is about to unfold momentarily.

Regret is now creating the tears forming in my heart but streaming from my lids as I muster with all my might not to make a sound. Unsurprisingly, the footsteps have stopped alongside my desk and I wait. Within a matter of seconds, I feel as though the back of my neck is being perforated with three sharp razors entering my flesh. "AHHHH," I scream at the top of my voice as I look up into the smiling face and eyes of Catarina, Cordell's daughter. Seeing my en-rag-ed eyes seems to delight her and her careless laugh spits venom in my face. She then shrugs her shoulders and twists on her heels heading in the direction of her seat but not before catching the whirlwind of this three-pound Language Arts book to the face. It is now she that is bewildered and spiraling towards the ground as I quickly spring from behind my desk.

I have become loose and explosive in 2.2 seconds and there is no turning back. I look upwards just in time to see Dawn from the corner of my eyes, making her way aggressively towards me. For this reason, Catarina's uncoordinated bestie is about to experience a double portion of my wrath. She throws the first blow and misses. This mishap excites me to a whole notha level and my insides are leaping.

After ducking to avoid being hit, I swing and imagine striking her with the brunt force of a mule kicking her. Immediately, I connect with her left kidney. She falls forcefully onto an empty desk and lands with the left side of her ribcage straddling the desk. The class is in an uproar of approval and cheering for more violence and bloodshed. The teacher has now deleted her attempts to peacefully intervene and is now frantically dialing the number for the Main Office. She has now delegated them to send the Resource Officer to room 312, in her words, "last week!" Depleted, she appears, as she cradles herself looking in the other direction altogether.

In my head, I unleash a blood curdling shriek, "TOO LATE!" I run back to Catarina who is laid out on the floor and kick her once more in the stomach before unleashing deliberate stomps to her face. One, for thinking that she is so much better than me. Two, and most crucial, is in appreciation of knowing that her punishment will deliver her father great pain. Three, for simply being too cute and girly for me to bare. At this very moment, I promise myself that neither she nor her father will forget this day. In turn, I will relive it as often as possible without one iota of regret.

All of a sudden, these kicks and stomps are not damaging enough. Hatred has multiplied like lead anchors in both my feet and spirit and I begin jump-dancing the spelling of my name onto her face. I am screaming with whaling arms at the cross roads in my life, trapped between destruction and insanity. I hear the marching feet of men rushing at me followed by muffled words. I am suspended in midair flailing aimlessly like some sort of wilder-beast. I am fuming and yet I am fire extinguished. I am hurt at the highest level com-prehendible and yet the arms that have torn me away from the fight I now find serenity within. I let out a wail that has been buried since birth and I cry uncontrollably onto his shoulder.

Chapter 3

This storm of rain has yet to stop ruining my parade. The clouds continue to trudge on behind me and yet it overshadows my view. Life continues to bless me with a pulse and yet categorically denies me any desire to live. I have been granted a voice however collectively I am muted. I hunger for love and therefore I am starvation daily for imaginary intimacies. Hope has been void as checks written from closed bank accounts and yet there is something which recognizes that one day I too shall rise—unfortunately, it won't be today...

Feeling elapses me as I sit silently in the Guidance Office wishing that I could mute my eyes and suffocate my ears. I am trapped within the screams of both victims and can't escape. I am taunted by the paralyzing power of unattempted possibilities and pondering how it is that I fell victim to such chaos. I become endlessly blank stares and vanishing is the person that I was an hour ago. Mental numbness, fatigue and despair envelope me in a harness predestined to fail.

Into a sleep-like trance I slip. I comprehend the world as doors closing tightly behind, in front of and upon me. I am the victor and yet I am devoured. I am strength and yet I am dissolved. Faintly, I hear Mrs. Johnson saying that they must follow the discipline matrix put in place by the Board of Education. This means that they are discussing the cause of the fight and tallying the damage versus my previous disciplinary records in order to configure an appropriate course of action.

Saturated with compassion, I hear the argumentative stance of Mrs. Johnson. "She has never been in my office for discipline in the two years that she has been here. As a matter of fact, she has been here constantly as the victim of bullying!" One irate voice transcends beyond the administrative offices and sends chills bubbling throughout my spine, "Well, alright then Sherlock! Has either one of those students been accused of such allegations?" Not nearly snappy enough, she struggles to sound confident, "I'm not sure about that, but I'm certain that this is merely her cry for help. No one that we've talked to today have any clue why this fight even began."

The male, dominant voice bites back again, "So, what would you suggest? Let's just sit here until your whys are answered! And what about the two victims that were carried out of here on stretchers? Do they not matter or is it that they simply aren't as important? What about the fact that their, as well as the other parents, trust their children in our care? Well, I'll tell you what, you can sit here and play scratch and sniff all you want but I unlike you, I'm going to do my job."

The door tears open and I twirl my eyes upward as the Resource Officer pulls the shackles from behind his back. He demands that I stand to my feet. I blink. Mrs. Johnson, running behind him interjects and asks him to wait until she contacts my mother. Looking me in the eyes with the harshest glare ever and totally ignoring her, he mandates, "To your feet now!" I swallow. He pulls me up and turns my face to the wall. I faint…

I wake to find myself face down, bound in the back of a speeding patrol car heading south both emotionally and literally, full of shame. I remain silently glued to the dried-up saliva on the backseat. I listen endlessly to the conversation between the male and female officers. It seems as though they speak for an eternity about things that are absolutely meaningless. They float from one topic to another without pause. The kids, spouses, finances and family trips seem to be the reoccurring themes.

My pride is trampled and the beating of my heart feels as though it is sharp enough to pierce through my t-shirt. The vehicle slows and I notice a darkness casting a shadow over both the roof and my window. I focus on it as we glide over a bump and slowly rock into a parked position. This appears to be the first time that the two have taken notice of me that I'm aware of. I am an oblivion of loss. Lost thoughts, appetite, balance and time suppresses me.

The back door is now opened and I am hurried toward the entrance of the building. Their lips move fervently and then flat line as if a question has been posed. I question mark them back with my empty stare. Stopping suddenly, I take an exaggerated glance around the garage concentrating on the ceiling. Hell, it only seems natural as it is what houses each of us in totality at this very moment. I recall Mrs. Seiko's promises that "the sky is the limit" pertaining to my future. Yet again, I have fallen excessively short.

Once more, I am nudged and submit willingly to do what is required and continue walking. Ironically, I enter into the back of the building face first. I am being led by the female officer as she continuously piers over her shoulder trying to gauge whether or not I am alright, present or conscious. I find myself alternating between being pulled forward and perfect stillness as I attempt to absorb my new surroundings. Everything looks dingy, dirty and disgusting which ignites a heightened sense of alert and alarming lack of trust for these peculiar people in my presence.

My inquisitive nature is more like dead weight until I spot a new set of mischievous eyes trying to pier right through me. I look away as she steps closer and introduces herself as Officer Tigner. She explains the order of events that will take place. She also informs me that due to my age, I will eventually be placed into the Bullpen by myself or with other juveniles as I am now property of the County Jail. In that same breath, she divulges the fact that since my arrest was on a Friday, I will not have my "hearing" in court until Monday. After this renegade of announcements, I had to determine whether or not I was on the world's worst Fear Factor ever or just plainly being punked!

Seemingly unfazed by my frustration, she smoothly shifts forward in the process. She asks the normal line of questioning: name, age, and birthdate, so on and so forth. I have gladly responded to none of her questions which leads the officers to talk among themselves as if I am not in the room. Officer Tigner's look now puzzles me as I am not sure whether she is concerned or ticked off. She is now requesting my parents contact information as if that changes something. Handing her the manila folder from the school office, the male officer begins explaining the events of earlier today as if he was an eye witness himself.

Haaa! You would swear that this dude knew me personally the way that he splurges on all the detailed wrong answers he's giving. She looks back at me once more. Never saying a word aloud, which makes me even more uneasy. I am not sure what she is thinking or feeling but it looks painful as her pen explodes upon her documents. Before you know it, I am fingerprinted, photographed, undressed, redressed and placed in another holding cell. Alone.

Although my appearance is that of someone alone, afraid and incarcerated, I can hear the commotion ringing out from beyond the concrete walls surrounding me. Separating me from it and the others is my silence, desperation and disbelief. Behind these bars lies utter confusion and cold that swells my heart with regret. Time passes as the stillness consumes me. Two food trays have been offered. Both remained untouched until recollected. I slumber while wide awake. Collapsed upon a mattress of brick, I drift between my past and present for my future is not yet guaranteed. The thought and presence of this cage strangles me into a restless sleep.

Chapter 4

I travel in and out of the darkness like a light flickering on and off in a child's playroom. I am present in the absence of mind and bodily activity. I am the very essence of not, and my self-worth has dwindled to even less. Temporary silence both comforts while detaching me from the bitter reality challenging me. The absence of light both smiles upon my person while simultaneously stabbing me in the face. I can't eat, feel or pretend to desire this life any longer. I chase objects throughout the night to assist in my exiting of hell's grip. My soul cries out to my mother and her negligent ways. Feeling at this moment as the lowest point staining this earth. And then I hear a voice kissing me from within say, "Even in your darkest hour, I am the light. Stop calling out to man and call upon me and I will provide for all of your needs!"

If I can best describe how I felt emerging from the darkness surrounding me, it would be comparable to a deep-sea diver rushing to the surface grasping for much-needed air. I am catapulted meeting that very surface with a sun-sized headache and tubes entering and exiting my body like stitches. My eyes race back and forth searching for familiarity and comfort. Neither am I faced with presently. Emptiness stares back at me and fills my person with gloom. Faintly, I hear frantic whispers growing louder and bolder. I try to sit up but can't. I am tied down in what resembles a simulated infirmary.

My bed is soft as rose petals but the smell of sickness is thick in my nostrils. My eyes begin sweeping every inch of my confines as my ears tune up slowly to the whispered chattering in the corner of the room. The beeping of my machines begins chirping aggressively. I lay still and repeatedly count the empty beds in an effort to seize the fear multiplying within. Out of nowhere or so it would seem, my eyes are staring back into a glazed over set of friendly brown eyes fixed upon mine. Without uttering a singular word, she takes her hand and smoothly brushes the loose hairs from my forehead. She confesses that she has been waiting for me.

In a low tone she asks, "How are you doing my love?" and patiently waits for a response. It appears that I have lost my voice due to the emotions swelling in the back of my throat. Slowly, I turn my face and eyes towards the beeping and back towards her. As if on cue, she lifts her hands and silences the ruckus between us. This moment is delicate and naturally nurturing. The silence compliments how I feel. Another nurse briskly enters the room. Her eyes are fixed on the machines in the corner as Edith raises her hand and announces just above a whisper, "I got it, sweetheart." Without missing a beat, the other nurse, swivels and twist out of the door just as quickly as she entered.

My attention is now glued to my new-found hero and I am hoping that she will never have to leave my side. There is something mystical about her personality and something magical about her touch. She is sincerity's portrait and kindness defined. Seemingly, she is here for me and I devour every second in her presence. Her eyes are simply as soft as expensive pillows and I feel overwhelmed with every sort of emotion, yet, not so alone, unworthy or discarded. I look at her and imagine that she understands not only how I feel but who I am as well.

Laying here, I marvel at the grace displayed in her every movement as she completes my assessment. I feel as if love has climbed onto me and wrapped its arms around me tightly. I have shed every negativity in the past hour like detox and feel a chill followed by goose bumps engulfing me from the top of my head to the souls of me feet. There is a presence that I cannot name nor see but can feel heavily permeating the atmosphere. I am perplexed at the irresistible sense of urgency to do the ugly cry. For no reason at all, I wale until I am emptied...

As the tears stream from Edith's eyes, she begins to sing softly. My room is peaceful yet electric. The love expressed is comprehended, impenetrable and tangible. She then asks my permission to pray. My swollen eyes jolt open and I am momentarily mortified. That unfamiliar inner voice says, "Fear not my child."

In one smooth seamless motion, Edith drops all that she is doing, continues humming the sweet melody and waltzes back over to my side. She then uses the remote for the bed, places me in a sitting position and loosens my restraints. Repositioning herself on the left side of my bed, she then hugs me tightly and begins rocking me as if I was her very own infant. She opens the prayer by thanking her Heavenly Father for all that he has done for us. *What? Wait a minute!*

I want to buck loose as I have a lot not to be... she continues as if she didn't notice my knee-jerk reaction. She then asks for forgiveness for anything that we have done, said or thought that hurt HIM or any of his children. Instantly, I think of the girls that landed me here and I explode into her arms. Inwardly, I am screaming. "I'm so SORRY!" My body is trembling but so is hers. This is nothing like anything that I have experienced before. With each tear that I shed, I feel not only cleansed but weights being lifted and battles being won.

Without shame nor traces of regret, I melt. Like the unwanted damaging layers of my life being unfolded calmly and carelessly. I am exposed. I feel like intentional nakedness presented on an empty, beautiful, exotic beach. With arms open and raised toward the sun smiling back upon me, I feel acceptance and reassurance in her hug. I am renewed and no longer confined by my anger and chained to my hurt. It feels as though the struggle has been silenced, fears are collapsed and healing is seemingly authenticated.

I am folded not only physically but emotionally as I am induced into a coma-esque sleep that quickly renders me incognizant of time, place or current situation. I am helplessness in her arms until I am no longer. Uncertain when or how it occurred, however, I experience the best sleep ever. Never moving, or so I think, stillness becomes my refuge and the serenity of my dreams. I am peace—until I am torn apart by angry, snarling lions encircling me in my dream turned nightmare! I scream myself awake as a cold intense sweat consumes my body…

Chapter 5

Your emotional abuse I have depended on like a crutch. Now that you are no longer here, I am at the totality of loss at every angle imaginable. I don't know who I am without you and yet I remain defeated in your presence. Without you, it seems that I cannot be me. With you I am likened to the LIGHT being strangled out by darkness. It's moments like these that I feel as bare as a stripped car abandoned in an unfamiliar location. I am comparable to its owner looking for the only key to salvage my lost transportation, unaware of the uselessness due to the vehicles current condition. I wander from one day to the next like a lost child void of IQ, needing guidance, protection and loving intentions to nestle upon. It isn't until now that I begrudgingly realize that it cannot nor will it ever be you. I hate you as I love you simultaneously...

Her name tag says Nancy and the frown that she wears hammers fine lines across her face like angry road maps. She is taking notes as she asks each question. I now realize that I am the subject of each sentence and the adjacent proper noun is Magdalana Moore, my mother. The issues at hand are (1) her absence; (2) reluctance to respond to court-ordered deadlines; (3) the old bruises and scarring covering my body; and (4) my mother's negligence to attempt to find out about my whereabouts. All of this spells trouble engraved in all caps. The questions swiftly sweltering in my head are "For whom?" followed by "Now what?"

Feeling light-headed and as if I were trapped in a funnel, my breathing increases as the machine rings to life with her annoying chiming. Both sets of eyes dart wildly back in my direction as if an immediate admission of guilt was fastened upon their faces. As dark as it is on my side of the room, I know that they not only can feel my eyes penetrating them both but also see my amplified stare shouting back at them through the darkness. Nancy frantically shuffles to my side. Apologizing as she presses the call light, she then pulls on the cord which produces an all too aluminous light.

Just above a whisper, she says, "You are alright honey. Just take a deep breath." But I can't. Her look, trembling hands and cantankerous breath, mirror how I feel which bothers me tremendously. And I wish, with ALL of my might, that she would simply back up out of my personal space! Her breath is as offensive as two closed fist meeting your best smile as your first greeting in the morning! I wish that I had the power to bottle her breath and hurl it back into one of her nostrils so that she can be doubly as offended as I am right now.

Even with the unwanted light blaring just above the head of my bed, I still feel dark. Edith glides into my room seamlessly or as if she had never left, humming a light melody. She locks her eyes into mine as if a commandment to be still, breathe light and focus on her. She cancels the call light and my fears quickly although she and everything else appear to be moving in an intensely slow motion.

Inadvertently, my breathing mimics her singing instantly or so it seems. I relinquish my rights and allow my mind to drift. Currently, I am wondering if Edith could sense me from afar seemingly losing control or if she was anticipating my need and in clear view of my call light? Synonymously, I feel like Alice of Wonderland, falling through the rabbit's hole of excessive anxiety being housed within my chest. Gratefully, that feeling has dissipated and I am waiting to see what will now take its place. I look up at Edith with fragile forlorn eyes. She gently asks the Social Worker to leave us. I ask her to pray for and with me once again.

Shortly thereafter, I turn to reposition myself in bed. I glance out of the barred window in the center of the room and pause. I see a rainbow smiling upon me. It appears to be at arm's length in distance and well within my grasp. It glistens; the colors are soft yet boisterously charismatic. In the rainbow, I sense life as it was intended to be—light yet abundant. I am saturated in a mixture of unabridged emotions. I smile as my heart rejoices knowing with clarity that some powerful changes are in progress. I allow the tears of joy to stutter onto my face. Subconsciously, I sense a break which stimulates a much needed release and sigh! Tranquility not only fills my person, it penetrates and engulfs my room.

Even the white walls surrounding me appear to be moving outwardly in fashion as I lay peacefully in this sterile bed. I shovel the rest of my cold, bland breakfast down towards the back of my throat. As if entangled in an endless sea of motionless thoughts, I am shifting while I remain glued to the same place in my mattress and meditation. I have concluded that self-reflecting is needed. Contrarily, I continue to draw a blank wild card lacking both color and creativity. My eyes appear transfixed and emptied as my mind is weighted.

I feel trapped, trampled, torn and impartial. I feel silenced and unplugged from reality. I am confusion whirling unequivocally internally and appear plastered externally. I pause and remind myself to breathe. *Just relax*, I say softly choking back the raw emotion convicting my spirit man to erupt violently in order to mask my unveiled vulnerability. I hear, "No weapon formed against me shall prosper," three times before I spit it out reluctantly.

Longing for freedom from the powerful, invisible chains that bind me to an ill temper and course actions. I refrain which sends a ceasefire to all channels connecting in my brain. It isn't until now that I see a bright new outfit laying at the foot of my bed. I get ready to pounce in this romanticized moment and then betrayal comes for me swinging its sharp sword. Instead, I anxiously await finding out the reasoning and occasion. Wondering where I will be heading today, instantaneously, I dismiss the thought.

My reality concludes that no one, namely my missing mother, Mag-Gie, would have done such a thing for me. Surely, the clothing must have accidently landed on the wrong bed this morning. I am more than certain that this mix up will inevitably be corrected before the days end. Thus, there is no real reason for me to get set up with the hopes for excitement only to be let down by disappointment which my days have generally brought about in the past.

I close my eyes both slowly and tightly in an attempt to remove all negativity. The singular problem that I am faced with is the fact that I can still hear myself thinking in waves and circles. Something within me craves "more" but I am unaware of what. I feel as though I have been stranded mid-thought and I experience a feeling similar to déjà vu, except opposite. This moment is original, sporadic and not remotely like anything I have ever experienced before. I have a heighted sense of awareness, I think. As time transpires, I am aware of every semi-second in passing.

Several hours pass. My breakfast tray is collected as I view three people huddling just outside of my door. Apparently, their morning meeting has concluded. Nancy, a nurse and her assistant enters the gateway of my room. The nurse begins knocking apprehensively as they all enter un-invited. I raise to a seated position without a word. I place my chin on my right hand's knuckles and lean on the tray table—waiting.

They all glance among each other. Silence, followed by palpable heart beats and fluttering eye blinks. I continue to watch as they stare aimlessly. I am screaming on the inside, *WHAAT*, but attempt to play it cool and tap my fingers as lightly as my aggressive heart would allow.

They remain the shutterers before me at a loss for words. They appear to be united merely by the blankness unleashed by their confused stares which seem to be aimed at but not driven into my eyes. The nurse has now physically regrouped and goes over to the window. She opens the blinds and asks how my breakfast was. I roll my eyes and repeat "Breakfast" like it hurt my tongue to say it.

At this point, I am highly annoyed with some expletives attached in my head. The other two shift nervously. "Well", she says. Did you see the clothes at the foot of your bed?" as she nods towards them.

I simply reply, "I did." I give her a haughty stare which causes another to take over the conversation. "Look, Destiny. There is no easy way to tell you this, but today is going to be a big day for you. This is why the social worker brought in these new clothes for you." In wishing that they would speed up the *bad news* process, I ask with a single word, "For?"

Simultaneously they chime, "Court…"

Chapter 6

As I walk into the courtroom, I see a room full of censorious eyes beaming at me. They are aligned with hatred and jam-packed with judgment. As they stare, I feel a chill creeping slowly down my spine and feel hesitant to move. I am wondering if my public defender will stand loyally by my side while working aggressively to redeem me. Will he/she even remember my name without glancing back onto the documents placed before him? Even if I were to win this case and am awarded liberation, will my spirit be free or will I persevere as the guilty as charged for a lifetime? Will my sincere apology help them to forget the horror that they all experienced or witnessed on that day? In this place, at this very moment, is any one of us innocent or are we simply a multitude of trapped souls waiting to point the finger? Quite frankly, it appears that I am the *monster* staining this room and I concur. My past actions speak louder than any words that I can muster in my defense. My anger had multiplied and manifested destruction which I can never reverse nor deny. I remain reluctantly glued to and repeatedly relive that moment that forever changed my life daily, "I'm sorry…"

You gotta be kidding me! is all that I'm thinking as she continues to purge her version of the truth on the stand. Knowing the total situation that landed me here in this very moment and yet it still seems so unfair and one-sided. Clearly, they are the victims and I have become the public display of monstrosity at its best. It's amazing to me how each witness can recall quote on quote, everything, like photographic poetry but has seemingly forgotten to mention the screams that escaped from this "wilderbeast" that triggered the fight to begin with.

I tap my public defender on the shoulder to enlighten him on this and he has the audacity to swipe my hand away. This seems so unfair and them-sided that I could just punch my own self in the face literally. And if this is not bad enough, Mr. Slippery, himself, proceeds to shush me which takes me to a whole new level of pistivity. The part that makes my inside explode is the fact that all that I can do in my defense is to sit still, in silence, with stupidity stapled to my face.

As I recall, on that particular day in question, it was never my intention to go into class and lay hands on anyone. As a matter of fact, I distinctly remember that MY focus was to refrain from any course actions or reactions. But for some strange, unknown reason, people (like nature) will never let me be at peace. They never stop pulling on me until I push back at them with an eruption-like force. Conversely, the jury, courtroom officials, judge, and onlookers will never know this or hear my voice explaining why I had to river dance on those two troublemakers because my PD has determined that I will not be speaking at these proceedings. This not only truly devastates me but it also leaves an immense taste of defeat throughout my person. *Who will hear my truth or side of the story as only I could tell it? Who will ever trust me, after hearing their rehearsed rendition of events if I cannot defend myself in this perfect setting?*

Feeling as if my rights have been alienated yet again, I commence to grinding my teeth and pretend to listen attentively. *My God! What have I done or allowed to transpire to deserve such radical treatment as this. Who truly decides our fate?* I would hate to believe that the universe has dealt this hand to me in an accordance that I am unfamiliar with and for reasons that I am uncertain of.

Well, whatever the reason, I have come to the realization that I have assisted them in painting me as the mongrel in this story. Whether knowingly or not, I have almost single handedly shredded any valiant laudable characteristic that I possess. It appears that this semi-second of a glitch (in life terms) has become the determining and defining sum of who I am. I am both overwhelmed and consistently offended during this array of floggings also known as trial. I remain semi-alert but full of fury from the beginning to the end of the proceedings. I would prefer to be tied to the back of a truck and drug for miles than to sit suffocating in silence while shots are being fired at me from within the courtroom.

With that being said, I glance back over my shoulder once again and watch as my hopefulness turns to remorseful and pathetic. The answer blaring in my head now is, nope! Not one familiar, compassionate eye is poised in my peripheral. This is seconded by another harsh nope. My mother has a lack of presence presently.

As I attempt to recuperate from this, my Public Defender, Jarvis Sham, nudges me with his shoulder which signals me to face forward during this malicious assassination of character. I have become a multitude of emotions but not one of them is admirable, appreciative or benevolent. I feel as though I have been hammered with razors in this stage play of a courtroom. However, not one person has attempted to stop the bleeding in this massacre nor have they pretended to care or take notice. Suddenly, I feel like there is a HUGE plunger sucking and draining the air out of my lungs as Caterina is sworn in.

I wake up, back in bed, drowsy and staring out of the same barred window as before. The last thing that I am aware of was Caterina standing before me with her right hand raised, the other positioned on the bible as she began to repeat after the sheriff. Even though that was damning enough, there was something even more disturbing than that. I could feel Cordell's aggressive eyes both penetrating and setting fire to my back before I turned around and confirmed it...

Chapter 7

What chances have I at survival in a world so cold and intent on my permanent plunder? Raining tears and worry I have tasted repeatedly but have never experienced unbounded love or joy. Never protected or shielded from seen or unseen blatant forces opposing my birth and pursuit for happiness. Repugnance I view in my reflection daily but it is not nearly as vile as the reality that I am faced with today. The hangover from yesterday's proceedings is congruent with the fact that I am at war continuously in this life. Both hands are tied behind my back, both legs are bound and duct tape is fastened over my lips. Yet you expect me to win like I have never tasted loss. My question is simple. *How?* The fight was fixed. I am the declaration of the opposite of win. I am not only at but defined as lost. I am exposed to a grilling chill. Then "the voice" says firmly, calmly "This battle is not yours…"

I sense the consummation of hate heavily concentrated and palpable in this room, centrally located at the core of this unremarkable building masked with the badging of guaranteed honor and justice. And somehow, I object to both. Equivocally, I am subjected to and reassured of much less. I have been told that justice is blind and I concur. To my recollection, it is the current twisting of truths, jabs thrown and successfully landed. It is lies lathered with the exaggeration of pretenses followed up more devastating blows and apparent amnesia. I sit swallowed in totality by speechlessness and yet I cast a shadow bigger than the totality of the people situated in this room.

Hypothetically, of course, if someone was to ask how I felt in this moment, I would have to say that I feel evaporated. It's as if I am present and yet the state of my being easily goes undetected due to the tarnished lenses provided by the prosecutor's witnesses. I have been repeatedly depicted as a ravenous monster or a devouring wolf caught in the hen's nest. Sadly, if the truth was broadcasted everywhere on loud speakers or even CNN, no one could be paid to believe that I am a sheep lost in wolf's clothing...

About the Author

LaTrice Marie was born and raised in Toledo, Ohio. She has worked predominantly in the medical field for fourteen years as a CNA and LPN. She has also worked in the car industry for six years. With that being said, she has learned that her love for people was not only part of her make up but also perfectly paralleled to her purpose in this life.

It was at that time that she began to realize that she knew struggle, pain and poverty like the back of her very own hand. She began to acknowledge that poverty is not just a current living condition but in fact the sum of a belief system or lack thereof. Simultaneously, she began to believe that she possessed the power to overcome every circumstance that she faced.

Through the healing, deliverance and motivation of ministry, she began to realize that words are in fact life. For this reason, she began to change her dialect. She began to speak prosperity into every area of her life. She began to step out on faith so great that it made her appear insane at times. As a result, she experienced an increase in faith, wisdom, strength and joy!

Her dreams began to materialize as she began to understand that our faith is increased by the direct actions that we take in accordance to our faith. This is her first attempt to step out of the shadows into the light and the purpose of her creation. She has now concluded that we are indeed our brother's and sister's keepers and therefore a call into action is paramount.

CPSIA information can be obtained
at www.ICGtesting.com
Printed in the USA
LVHW111333271019
635469LV00001B/130/P